CLAIRE FREEDMAN ★ RUSSELL JULIAN

George's Dragon

SCHOLASTIC

The moment George looked into Sparky's big, friendly, purple eyes, he knew.

"That's the pet I want!" he said.

"What, that funny looking lizard?"
asked George's dad.
   "Sparky is a baby dragon!"
explained the pet shop man, but
George's mum and dad
did not hear.

**"Pleeeeease
can I have him?
It *is* my birthday!"**
begged George.

"I suppose lizards
aren't *too* much
trouble," agreed
George's mum.

And with a huge smile, Sparky leapt happily into George's open arms.

On the drive home, George and Sparky
read the leaflet from the pet shop.

Your Pet Dragon
Important Information

★ Dragons come in all shapes and sizes. Remember, a baby dragon will GROW.

★ Baby dragons are still learning how to fly. Remove all fragile objects. Crash landings are to be expected.

★ Dragons love to practise breathing fire. It is best to start small, ie, marshmallow toasting.

Beware: accidents will happen!

"What's in that leaflet?" asked George's mum.
"I hope lizards behave themselves."

George looked at Sparky, and
they both grinned.

Ta-da! At George's birthday party, Sparky lit all the candles on his birthday cake in one go!

And the week that followed was one big, happy adventure for George and Sparky.

Yo-ho-ho!

They played pirates. Sparky made a fantastic First Mate.

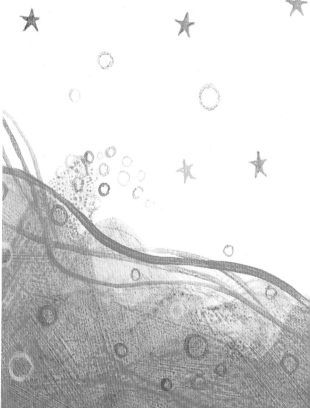

Yo-ho-ho!

He made an even better pirate ship.

Zoom!

They played astronauts.
Sparky was a brilliant space rocket.

But, best of all, they loved being together.

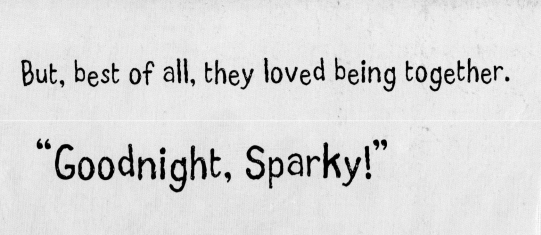

"Goodnight, Sparky!"

George said each night as he climbed under the covers.

"Snuggigooo!" yawned Sparky, from the foot of George's bed.

And neither of them had ever been happier.

But there was a problem. A growing problem.
"That lizard has grown HUGE!" gasped George's dad.
"He gets bigger and bigger every day!" George's mum sighed.

"All pets grow," said George. "You'll stop growing soon – won't you, Sparky?"
Sparky breathed in and tried to look smaller.

He let his breath out...

WHOOOSH!

... and accidentally singed the curtains. "That's another thing," grumbled George's mum. "Everything's covered in scorch marks."

"Sparky doesn't mean to do it," George said. "Do you, Sparky?"

"**Nooohotblott!**" squeaked Sparky, and he hung his head in shame.

But things got worse ... much worse!

SNap! Everything he sat on, he broke.

Oops!

Every time he got excited, he flew – usually too high,

SIZZLE!

Whenever he tried to help, he set something on fire. Sparky was a disaster zone!

"If things don't improve," said George's mum,
"it's back to the pet shop for him."

"Never!"
cried George,
hugging Sparky tightly.

"Noopynoozzz" whimpered Sparky sadly.
They could not bear the thought of being apart.

So Sparky tried extra hard to be good.
He helped with some dusting.

Crash!

Smash!

He helped bring in the newspaper, but that didn't go very well either. And trying to dry the washing was a terrible mistake!

"ENOUGH!" shouted George's dad. "Sparky goes back to the pet shop this weekend!"

"But Sparky *has* to stay," George pleaded. "He's my best friend!"

A huge purple tear slid down Sparky's scaly cheek. But George's parents' minds were made up.

The next morning, though, something out of
the ordinary happened. The car wouldn't start.
"How will I get to work?" worried George's mum.
"How will I do the shopping?" fretted George's dad.

"This is your big chance, Sparky,"
George whispered. "Just be very, very careful."

"Hoppyteehee!" giggled Sparky.
George's dad had never enjoyed shopping so much!

George's mum had a big grin on her face
when she came back home that evening.
"Sparky's been so helpful today," George's dad beamed.

"He's been wonderful," agreed George's mum.
"He really is a lovely lizard."

"Does that mean Sparky can stay?" George asked hopefully.
George's mum and dad nodded.

"Yipppee!"
yelled George.

"Duperboomboom!" whispered Sparky, being careful not to open his mouth too wide.

And from that day on, Sparky was an extremely well-behaved dragon...

Most of the time!

THE END